good deed rain

This is
the author's 60th book.
Others include:
At the Edge of America,
The Sylvan Moore Show,
A Hundred Dreams Ago,
Walt Amherst is Awake,
and many more…

THE

WORRYS

The WORRYS © 2023
Allen Frost, Good Deed Rain
Bellingham, Washington
ISBN: 978-1-0881-2168-9

Cover & Illustrations: Tai Vugia
Title Lettering: Priya Shalauta
Cover Production: Priya Shalauta
Writing: Allen Frost
Quote: Homer, *The Odyssey*, book 17, line 290.
Lucretius, *On the Nature of Things*, book 2, line 548.
Apple: TFK!

And a hound that lay there raised his head and pricked up his ears. When he noticed Odysseus standing near, he wagged his tail and dropped both ears, but he no longer had the strength to move

—Homer

as they tossed about the universe, whence, where, by what force, in what manner will they meet and come together in that vast ocean, that alien turmoil of matter?

—Lucretius

The WORRYS

Allen Frost

Good Deed Rain ◊ Bellingham, Washington ◊ 2023

introduction

I wanted to make the Worrys a clan of villains causing trouble all over town. That's what Roald Dahl would have done and that would've been fun, but *The Worrys* quickly went in another direction. Once I thought of them as a family, I didn't want anything to go wrong.

Having spent some time on Earth, this time in America specifically, I've seen how fear has steadily puffed itself up bigger and bigger. Now it seems like the country runs on it like electricity. But it wasn't always that way, and there will be a time when our senses return.

For a while now, I've been mixing up the maps of old Seattle and Bellingham as setting for books. Why not? Streets, lakes, seas, memories are moveable. I used to love going to the Fun Forest at the Seattle Center. It disappeared with the 21st Century but I can bring it back. Presto! Here it is! I like to think there's a sort of B-movie studio where all these stories are being filmed and the sets reappear and the plots and characters move in and out like dreams.

A.F 2/2/23

1.

The Worrys are a family of weasels. They live under a truck muffler dumped in a ditch on 13th Street. They steal chickens and cats if they can get them. They'll steal more than that given a chance. That makes them sound terrible, but they live in a constant state of fear, where they're just barely getting by, and they have to do whatever it takes to survive.

2.

For instance, just yesterday Lila Worry told her son and husband, "I'm tired of living in a house that leaks when it rains, in a ditch that can flood. I don't like the roar of the cars on the road above. And sooner or later a dog or a child will hop down here and find us. Don't you think it's about time we found somewhere new? Don't you think we're better than this?"

3.

It's true, everyone deserves a good, safe place to live. It doesn't matter if you're a bird or a bramble, a stone on the beach, or a girl on the radio. Believe it or not we're all on this planet together and we're connected in ways you might not even know. Lila's wish was carried on the late summer wind. Her voice was sent miraculously to the far reaches and like every prayer, it deserved to be heard.

4.

Jack Worry heard it and he had heard it before. That song was old as violins. When he left their home at dawn, it played in his head as he started his work, following the path he took every day, searching the side of the road, the dark swale of blackberry where the mice would hide. He hummed the same tune as always, prosperity is just around the corner, there like a kite in a tree, if only you could reach it.

5.

That's exactly what drove them out of their house and into an oak. Jack came running back to the ditch and he woke them up. He told his family what he found stuck in the branches. It fluttered like a nesting bird. They had seen flying machines before, buzzing and sputtering from cloud to cloud, or way up high scratching a white scar in the sky. He said, "Here's one we can get to! Here's one we can fly!"

6.

It didn't take long to pack what they had into a suitcase and bags. "Mom!" said Jolly Worry, "Where will we go?" She held a skillet and bindle of things they stole from a dollhouse. They had done this before many times, a weasel's life never settled down. She pressed her son near and told him this time would be different, they would be in the air. They would see the entire world and they would find the perfect place to land.

7.

So little Jolly and Lila and Jack Worry scurried out of the ditch and looked both ways before they crossed the road. Every animal learned the dangers of 13th Street. Lila squeezed her son's hand as they ran to the other side. A hidden rabbit eating a clover twitched her long ears and watched them. Birds were singing, the grass hissed with dew, they were in a big town that was just starting to waken.

8.

The rabbit stopped munching a green stem. You don't see a weasel family race past you every early morning, carrying their belongings. They disappeared into the next thicket and the rabbit listened to them as they disturbed the leaves and branches towards the cedar fence in someone's backyard. When she couldn't hear them anymore, the rabbit returned her attention to the sweet tasting flowers growing all around her.

9.

"How much further?" Jolly panted. They were stopped by a tall red wooden wall. It went up, up into the purple clouds. Jolly hoped they didn't have to climb it to get to the airplane. Where did planes go when they weren't flying? Did they ever rest on the tops of fences to sing with the birds until some urge made them take to the sky again? That's what a starling would do—was a plane any different?

10.

"Here it is," Jack Worry said. His hands running along the cedar planks found the loose board that could swing aside like a door, just big enough for them to slip through. He warned them, "We need to be very careful and quiet and fast." That was nothing new to Lila and Jolly, they were that all the time. Then he told them something that made them want to freeze to this spot like two weasel trees, "There's a dog on the other side."

11.

For a moment imagine there is a creature thirty-feet-tall, big as a dinosaur, that can rush at you across the lawn, snapping sharp teeth, that only wants to catch you and rip you apart. At night you may think you're safe in your bed, but there's a bark in the distance and another one answers, closer. Someone as small as Jolly Worry can only pull the blanket over and pray.

12.

Ever so carefully, Jack Worry pushed on the slat until he could edge his hand into the dangerous air of that backyard and look around. A rope was strung high above the ground and from it hung pants and shirts and socks and enough other clothes to fit four people standing guard. All the grass was a piranha lake they had to cross. The other side seemed a mile away. "Okay," Jack whispered, "the coast is clear."

13.

Or was it? The seat chained to the swing-set creaked in the creeping, rising breeze. Each new step they took rattled blades of grass. Lila pushed on her son, but he had seen something that made him halt. Noises came from the house. A thump, a metallic squeal, muffled voices. The kitchen window roared with yellow light. "Come on, Jolly!" his mother hissed and she dragged him by the backpack after the blur that was Jack.

14.

For the Worrys, fear is here, fear is there, fear is waiting, bristling everywhere. They were always alert, every sense taut as piano wire, connected to the idea that *something* is lurking, out to get them. They ran for their lives to the next hiding place. A crowd of ferns and shadows. There was no dog. Fear is a thing where even if it's invisible, you think it's there.

15.

"We made it!" cried Mr. Worry. That was the riskiest part of their journey, or anyway so they supposed. Anything was liable to happen. Sometimes the very thing you worry about will happen, sometimes not. You never knew. That's why he was so relieved to be here, alive, that he kissed and hugged his wife and son. Before them lay the woods…then the fields where their airplane was waiting.

16.

By now it was no longer early, the sun was in the leaves and beaming down on them in rays and beyond the trees the roads were filling with cars going off to offices. The moon was gone but not all the night had followed it. There were creatures like the Worrys who jumped and twitched at the slightest sound, while there were others who didn't seem worried at all. One of those sat in the crown of an alder, too hungry to go to sleep just yet.

17.

The owl swung itself off its branch. It plummeted silently. Jack and Jolly weren't aware of it, but Lila was prepared. She knew the list of predators that hunted in the woods. Coyotes and foxes were bad enough, but she was on the lookout for owls. As soon as she saw one, she caught the sun on the shiny skillet and pointed the reflection at the swooping bird.

18.

The blinded owl crash-landed in the leaves giving the Worry's enough time to escape. They were soon in the green weeds of the field. "How did you manage that?" said Jack, "I didn't know it was there!" Jolly piped up, "Neither did I!" Lila said, "I was thinking of all the things that could go wrong and all the things that are after us. That owl didn't surprise me, I was ready for him. See how it pays to worry!"

19.

Fortunately, the stalks of grass, bunched as a bamboo forest, kept them hidden from the air. No owl, hawk, kestrel, or eagle would dive in after them...Probably. "We're nearly there," Jack promised. Puffing along between them, Jolly said, "Next time I'm taking a taxi." At that, Jack and Lila were able to laugh and the sound was like water poured in an empty, thirsty cup.

20.

The oak tree was waiting for them. Jack pointed at their red and blue flying machine parked in the branches. Up where the birds made nests and songs, where if you didn't have wings you would fall. From where they stood, the tree looked like a big hand full of leaves—if only it would bend and lift them up and save them the trouble of climbing to the top of its green fingers.

21.

There was still plenty to worry about as they knitted through the undergrowth. Jolly couldn't help thinking about the deadly boa constrictor, how it could wrap its coils tighter and tighter around you until it squeezed out your very last breath. A weasel would be nothing but a wilted memory of life. Then it was down the hatch, swallowed whole. The anaconda was just as bad. The cobra's poison could knock out an elephant.

22.

At the base of the oak tree, a raccoon awaited them, striped fur bundling like the uniform of a doorman at a big-city 5-star hotel. Behind him was an entrance in the knotted wood. That could be the way to a marble lobby and an elevator running up through the trunk. Oh, I hope that's true, thought Lila, I've dreamed of places like this, and the thrill felt real as she tucked her skillet and worries away.

23.

Jack greeted the raccoon and explained they were here to fly away. The raccoon seemed a little slow to understand but once he did, he grinned and said, "Yes, yes, you're right on time. Leave your baggage with me and we'll make sure it get loaded for your departure." Two more raccoons appeared from the hole in the tree and the Worrys handed them their suitcase and bags and Lila's bindle of things.

24.

Not one of the Worrys suspected a thing while they scurried up the side of the tree, on bark that formed a stairway. No elevator, thought Lila, but this is fun, round and round and up and up. Jolly laughed as she chased after his tail. Then Jack told them, "Here we are!" and they stopped spinning at the start of a branch that led like a hallway. At the end, perched in the leaves with a long silk tail tangled in and out, was a terrific looking kite.

25.

Of course the Worrys had spotted airplanes before, never more than a toy or birdlike speck in the sky. There was no end to the machines that people created to creep and thunder and zip around in. They thought they owned the world and anything they made was an improvement. Most often, the safety of other animals was the last thing on their mind. The Worrys ought to have been wary when they decided to fly.

26.

For a weasel who has never been near a kite, it was strange indeed. They almost believed it was a sort of living creature the way the breeze made it breathe. Ms. Worry held her son close as Mr. Worry inspected the kite. Could it be like a flying carpet they were meant to sit on? It strained, ready to go. Then, "Look!" the boy said, figuring it out, "It's holding to the tree with its tail!"

27.

A possum will do that when it needs to reach a plum. A tail can be a wonderful, useful thing for an animal. So the weasels set to work untangling it from all the twigs. The kite was pulling more, it wasn't just the wind, it seemed hungry, like a trapped creature, knowing it was about to be freed. To the north the clouds were building, stacking and boiling and rolling closer over the land, across the field.

28.

The three weasels looped the long kite tail around themselves. Jack said make sure you're tied tight and don't let go! They had no idea where their next destination would be, but they were sure it had to be better than a truck muffler in a ditch on 13th Street. "What about our luggage?" Lila suddenly remembered. Where were those raccoons? Jack realized he forgot to worry about that.

29.

We'll just have to wait with our worries, Lila decided. She was wrapped in blue silk like a mummy, spun like a cocoon with her husband and son to the biggest butterfly she had ever seen that was testing its crackling wings, a hundred feet off the ground. What could go wrong? "I just want you to know," she said, "I love you both very much and I know wherever we go, we're together." Those were the last words she said in the oak tree.

30.

When a rollercoaster starts, it gives a lurch, a violent clack as the wheels bite the track, with a shaking noise like snapping branches as the pull of some unseen force throws you back. You might close your eyes in a moment of fear as the speed increases, or laugh into the roar of the world going by. It's happening so fast, suddenly you're dipping and swerving and climbing like a bird. The Worrys were in the air!

31.

Every summer ends with the wind. In August it stirs and sidles and wades in the air, then in September it becomes a cool breeze, gentle as a cat rubbing against the trees until the green leaves begin to loosen just a little. It's only a whisper, loving what the warm months have done to the world, decorated it with flowers and soft days and nights. When the wind turns cold, winter is on the way.

32.

October took the Worrys soaring high above town. "Look!" said Jack, "There's our house!" But Lila couldn't open her eyes, not yet. If anything happened it was a long, long way to fall. "Look at the water!" chirped Jolly, "Look at the hill!" Lila tried for a second to casually see what a bird must see, but it was too much. She was a creature of the ground and that's where she wanted to be.

33.

The kite was happy to be in the sky, this is what it was made for. Although the person who put its sticks and strings and pretty cloth together probably never expected there would be three weasels wrapped in its long tail, the kite was doing just fine. It carried its passengers smoothly, found an airstream that flowed like the creek in the ditch, a peaceful meandering, a feeling you could fall asleep to if you wanted to.

34.

The kite had no pilot, none that could be seen, it was unknown what steered it, who pulled the strings, or where the Worrys would go. They hoped to arrive in some perfect place—they each had their own ideas—like the colorful posters in a travel shop—Lake Lucerne, Tahiti, Shangri-La. When the town below them was obscured by cloud, they were taken up higher yet until they were set like a jewel in a blue sky over everything.

35.

Poor Lila was finally able to unlock her eyes. It wasn't bad, in fact it was beautiful. They were floating in place between a never-ending blanket of white clouds and a deep blue heaven. A whole other world was living in those clouds. The Worrys saw mountains and valleys, forests, oceans, towns like the one they came from, nested in the cumulus.

36.

The life of a weasel is rarely one of calm. They didn't have long to admire the dream they were in. Four dots had spotted them and were headed their direction. Jolly was the one who first noticed. By then the dots had grown wings. "Buzzards!" Jack hissed. Another bird on Lila's list of worries. She wished she had her skillet now. She almost wished they had never left home.

37.

The buzzards circled the Worrys lazily, the way they do on a hot sunny day when they search the fields and roadsides for a bite to eat. There wasn't much the weasels could do strung out like laundry on a line behind a kite. "What's going to happen?" Jolly asked. If only this was a story told to him at night, when they were safe in a rusted truck part and he was closing his eyes, just a few seconds from sleep.

38.

At the sight of danger, some hunted animals will freeze, as if by doing so they become an ordinary painting in a museum full of pictures you see then move on. Deer #302, anonymous, 18th century. The kite was like that, it had no intention of diving into the quilt of clouds, dragging the weasels along in its wake. It floated in place with weighted bait hooked to its eight-foot tail.

39.

Then it began. Like something Hemingway would have written. The first buzzard broke clean from the circling formation, wings turned back for speed, and when it hit, it was the way an arrow shot on a clear cold morning will strike its target with precision. A sharp beak tore across silk and separated Lila from her family. Bundled in knots, she fell like a pilot fumbling with a parachute.

40.

6,000 miles from this spot in the sky, a fourteen-year-old girl stands at a wooden table and her hands are a blur as she wraps together dowels, cloth and string, with a set of instructions. She has imagined the children in other lands running and laughing in the wind. While she works, she pictures America, Africa, the North Pole, the Amazon, Japan, and everyone has a kite that she made.

41.

But it's hard to believe that factory girl would have pictured the life and death of a kite in quite such a way as this. Shredded by buzzard claws and beaks, first one weasel fell off, then another, then the last. And while those rodents tumbled down out of sight, that kite she prepared, one of hundreds she assembled each day, was a crumple of silk and twigs batted by birds, falling into clouds.

42.

Back to Lila. What happened to her? She was terrified without a doubt, but she was also resourceful, especially when battling birds. Just ask that unfortunate owl from Chapter 18. In case you're wondering about him too, he's okay. Everyone in this book is protected. No matter what happens, or how bad it may seem, it's all part of the plan. We began this story with the Worrys together and we will end it with them together.

43.

What *did* happen to the owl? Now I'm curious too. Shall we just put everything on hold—leave the Worrys frozen for a minute, a thousand feet above the ground? There's a hole in a fir tree, halfway up the trunk, and if you stand on a tall ladder, you can look in. Careful, don't say a word. You don't want to wake him. He's asleep in bed, underneath blankets and a book, and he dreams of a happy night on the moon.

44.

Lila held on to the ends of tattered silk that hooped overhead making a puff of cloth parachute. She couldn't see Jolly or Jack. She yelled their names but the sky is a big place. If only they had made plans for this, but you can't know everything, there's only so many worries you can carry. "Jolly! Jack!" she shouted again. How far can a weasel's voice travel in the clouds? I'm not sure that's ever been tested before.

45.

Her arms were sore. She didn't know how much longer she could hold on to her parachute. The city beneath was built of concrete and metal and other hard things. Luckily there were also plenty of trees lining streets, in backyards, and she saw a park with more and there in the middle, a big green colored pond. She wasn't fond of water, but after all this dropping she needed something soft to catch her.

46.

Lila kicked her legs and steered with her tail and her navigation worked. She felt like an astronaut returning to the sea. Not that it was easy, there were currents and breezes that tried to pull her astray. "Go ahead," she told the turbulence, "You can't stop me." The pond was where she meant to be. She could worry about swimming when she got there.

47.

Two other parachutes drifted over town, probably too small for radar, probably too small to be seen by anyone going about their day. How often do most people stop to look at the sky anyway? It's beautiful and strange and ever changing. I suggest we all take a moment right now, right this second, to put this book down and go to a window or step outside and open yourself to the universe.

48.

Looking at the sky isn't just daydreaming. Whether it's the night stars or the weather movie that plays in the day, that open window to another world goes on and on. Who are we, looking out? No bigger than a spot on a moth wing. Another little bright light, another poppy seed. How brief we are, no more than a blink. Three small weasels fell from the sky like raindrops.

49.

Lila was the first to land. A splash in green water. The sound was like a salmon. Someone looked from the shore and saw where the splash sent out a ring of small waves creasing the pond. It fell from the sky, whatever it was, and lay on the shallows, waiting for him to wade out. It could be a thing worth having. His boots were already muddy, a little water would only wash them clean.

50.

The Blackberry Maniac lived in the park. Before you get the wrong idea, part of his name came from his house, a pile of blackberry vines ten-feet tall that ran for thirty-feet or so along the cement wall on the other side of the parking lot. He burrowed a tunnel into it like a rabbit. Would a maniac walk in a pond to save a drowning creature? Would a maniac carry her ashore and wrap her paw with bandage?

51.

Just after Jolly found himself falling, for just a second, he caught sight of his mother. He didn't know if it would be the last time. She was floating beneath a flower, one he knew he could make too by unravelling the kite remains he clutched. She showed him in a cartoon second what to do. He left his outline cut in a cloud as he dropped through and on the other side he was parachuting.

52.

Jolly saw more of the world than he ever knew. He had never ventured that far from the ditch on 13th Street and here he was looking at a planet that stretched out endlessly. He could aim for any direction. By pulling on his parachute, he could steer. It was fun, it became a game to slide this way and that in the air. But the fun only lasted until the cloth began to tear.

53.

Jolly had seen flying squirrels before in the wood near their house. One of them jeered at him as it soared overhead like a jay and little Jolly wished he could hold out his arms like that. He even dreamed that he could. Then for a few minutes his prayer came true, he was higher than any squirrel or raccoon or weasel (save for two). All he had to do was find somewhere safe to land.

54.

The last parachute carried Jack. When he saw the city below and no sign of the other Worrys, he knew they would be spread miles apart, torn from each other like the kite. He blamed himself, it had been his idea to fly and now they were in more trouble than they'd ever been. If only he could rewind time, if only he could start the morning again and stay in bed and touch Lila's shoulder again.

55.

If only he could...then something struck his parachute—were the buzzards back?—and he was enfolded in the plummeting broken remains of his flying machine. He couldn't see the ground anymore, the town rushing to meet him, he clawed his way into the ball of circus-colored cloth and waited like the hero of a cliffhanger movie to be safe in the next reel.

56.

My own father told me a story of long-ago New England days when he and his friends went to the Pastime Theatre on Main Street every weekend afternoon to see *King of the Rocket Men*. I could imagine being there too, in the dark with all the kids of town (before the future made this memory) the silver light, the atomic roar, holding our breath as Chapter 10 "The Deadly Fog" began to roll.

57.

Three weasels. Each Worry fell on a different part of town. Lila opened her eyes in a blackberry cathedral. Jolly bounced off a balloon and entered the Fun Forest. Jack emerged from kite wreckage on the Leopold rooftop. Each Worry was facing their own adventure and the mystery of what they would do next was as real as Rocket Man's next chapter.

58.

Lila opened her eyes. At least she wasn't falling anymore. She was steady, comfortable even, lying on her back blanketed in cloth with cardboard walls around her. It was a shoebox, padded with a flannel shirt. Her arm though—something was wrong—it was bound and splinted with a wooden matchstick and it hurt to move. Above her were leaves and vines that crisscrossed, cracks of blue sky.

59.

Houses and apartments are all over the city but not every person lives in one. Some live in cars, or tents, or curl up on cardboard wherever they can. It isn't easy to explain, not to a child, or a weasel with a broken arm. Except Lila wasn't scared, someone cared for her, someone brought her to this safe place which after all seemed a step up from a ditch on 13th Street.

60.

There was even electricity! The Blackberry Maniac—and really, he deserves a better name than that, soon—had patched a wire from a lamppost into the thorns and shadows so he could have light and a hotplate and the heater that was warming the shoebox. Lila was fine, she knew she was lucky, as if she had been rescued by a fairytale woodcutter.

61.

Luck was with Jack and Jolly too. People say luck to mean all kinds of things but really it just means someone is looking out for you. I've been protecting these weasels faithfully and three is quite a flock, especially now they're apart and I need to jump constantly from Lila, to Jolly, to Jack. It's a lot of work. If there are guardian angels, I suppose I can qualify for the job.

62.

Is that what I am, is that what I do? I've been given the task to care for three weasels, to see them through, and I've taken an interest in them and so apparently have you since you've made it this far. Now we're in it together, you and I, as long as I can keep their story going, and you keep reading, we will take the Worrys safely to the end of this book.

63.

Jack heard wings. Lots of them. He knew that sound from chasing chickens and hunting chickadees, but he never heard so many move all at once, all around him. He emerged from the wreckage of a disastrous flight into a weasel's dream-come-true. For a moment he was overwhelmed by all the eyes and all the bluish feathers. If he was younger and less wise, he might have gone berserk right then and who knows where he'd be.

64.

Yes, it was quite a scenario. A hundred pigeons were backed to the wall. He stepped free of the kite, saw the hole created in the ceiling above, saw the city towers wrapped around him with chicken-wire keeping him in. The cage door was firmly latched. Jack took another step and his fellow prisoners shuddered. A black tar rooftop. The drop. He could enjoy the finest feast of his life but then how would he get to the ground? Hmmm… he had to be clever.

65.

It was one of those classic puzzles. Jack would have to think his way through. His empty stomach growled. What should he do? He couldn't stay trapped. He drummed his hands on the taut wire cage. There must be someone who came to the roof to feed the prisoners, but if the jailer saw him, it would be goodbye Jack. He turned to the birds. If he harmed even one of the pigeons, he knew he would lose their help.

66.

Jolly also found himself with a problem to solve. Fortunately, the big blue balloon he bounced off saved his life—unfortunately, it sent him into the gnashing gears of the Bonanza shooting gallery. Of all the rides and games of chance at the Fun Forest carnival, this might have been the most dangerous for a weasel. Even the Windstorm roller coaster, with all its scares and bends and turns, is at least predictable.

67.

A streamer of kite tail trailed with Jolly as he sailed into the fairground machinery. He just missed a pop-up rabbit that could have batted him back, away from the cogs and chains behind the scenes. Like Charlie Chaplin, he ran on a factory wheel that took him up and down into the bright spotlights and blasting sounds and worst of all were the guns shooting at him.

68.

It's difficult to leave Jolly at this place in time,
let's just freeze it though and step back for a
moment. Lively as it seems, with crowds drawn
here all day and night, the Fun Forest is only a
dream. Everything you see, the bumper cars, the
Tornado, the Ferris wheel, the carousel, the Flight
to Mars, will be undone and folded up and sent
away. People will later say they saw the Pirate Ship
ride out on the bay, as it sailed from sight.

69.

Lila woke up to creaking, rocked back and forth, a seagull crying in the late afternoon blue above. She couldn't see over the carboard walls that surrounded her, only the ocean of sky. Another seagull floated by. She was no longer locked under leaves, she could hear the rush of cars, she was moving with them, beside a road. A busy one, not like back home. The seagull circled back, tipped a wing and noticed her.

70.

Allow me another digression by the author if you'll be so kind. The Fun Forest really did exist, although now it's only a spinning and shiny glimpse of old Seattle in memory. I couldn't recall the name of the shooting gallery—I had to ask my friend Aaron who was also a boy back then. He knew right away—Bonanza—it was a big word that puzzled him, attached to something unreal that eeled in the electric noise of night.

71.

Ragtime piano played by a slumping mechanical man with a tin pan target on his back. Animals, a green turtle, a turkey vulture, a skunk that raised its tail when hit, a cuckoo clock. Tin cans to knock over, a roulette wheel, skulls and moving targets. The loud snap of rifles and six-shooters and right in the middle of the Wild West was a young weasel named Jolly hiding behind a cactus.

72.

"Please don't think of me as your enemy," Jack told the pigeons. "I promise I'm not here to eat you. I only want to find my family. Believe me, I could use some friends with wings. If I let you out, could you look for them?" He had to put his hunger on hold. Jack knew the advantage of the air—when he was up there, he saw the whole world—one truth about weasels: their vision is sharp as their teeth.

73.

The Blackberry Maniac's name was John although he lost that years ago. He didn't need a name once he became like a bird living in the leaves and picking crumbs from the streets and alleys. He pushed a grocery cart. It held a memory too—of when it traveled aisles filled with an abundance of food for sale—like an animal used to a corral, it broke free and became less mechanical, a companion and keeper of treasure on the streets.

74.

Lila was one of those treasures. She rode in the cart like Cleopatra on the wake of the Nile. The sky looked onto her, no sign of her floating family in it, while the caster wheels turned on cement. Another dumpster lid fell shut and a hand offered her a peppermint. She tasted it. It was so sweet and fiery she turned her head away. "Sorry," the man said. Then the hand returned with a sandwich.

75.

Have you ever had a sandwich appear when you were like a weasel with a broken arm, pushed between trashcans, and all your worries about what will happen next have dragged you down low as you've ever been? A sandwich is something to savor, to be thankful for. Especially in these rare moments. There is nothing less imaginary than when miracles are portioned out.

76.

Another pellet zinged past Jolly. He could see them coming, fast as bees. He had just enough time to react and get out of the way. Wherever he tried to hide, a steam whistle or a bit of machinery would toss him back into view. None of the other animals seemed to mind getting shot—they just sat there and waited for it to happen. The only exception was the talking moose.

77.

A moose head was mounted on the wall not far from the piano. He looked at the line of people shooting and told them exactly what he thought of them. He scowled and rolled his eyes and swiveled his antlers and shook and each time he was shot, a bell would ring next to him. When you walked past Bonanza on your way to the Matterhorn ride, that bell pealed like a church in distress.

78.

If it wasn't for the moose, Jolly might have given up too. There was room for him to cower by the rabbit, but the moose made Jolly think of heroes who never surrendered. That voice guided Jolly over every obstacle. He leaped past the rabbit and a bottle that tipped and tried to pin him. He slid beside the piano and hid behind its leg. The moose brought him to safety, but it helped that none of the carnival guns shot straight.

79.

The Blackberry Maniac who wasn't a maniac and used to be John, stopped pushing his grocery cart. "I want to show you this place," he told Lila. He lifted the cardboard box and tipped it enough for her to see. "This is where I'm going to let you go. Tomorrow, when you're feeling better." The sun was getting low. It glowed in the layer of trees and spread the shadows across a yellow field of birds.

80.

The grocery cart swiveled on the crackly gravel as it turned around. Lila was happy in her shoebox with her broken arm—she had found her new home! All it took was falling from a plane. And all she needed to do next was find Jolly and Jack. That would happen, she was sure of that. Tomorrow. She closed her eyes and felt the rumble of the wheels on cement. Tomorrow they would be back together.

81.

The latch unclasped, Jack swung on the opening door, and out poured a flood of pigeons. All those wings knocked him to the rooftop. The bird cloud circled the Leopold building once while the pigeons set their compasses and plotted their course, then they were gone, whistling, flapping from sight. Jack went to the ledge and looked over the edge. The town spread far, from the bay into trees, and all he had was a pigeon promise.

82.

The Bonanza shooting never stopped for long. Jolly held onto the piano leg, wondering what to do next. The moose kept on talking, the bell kept ringing, the ragtime piano kept on repeating. Would this war ever end? Is this what people did for fun? They turned the world into scares. They could make things beautiful, but they always had this other side. Jolly wished he had landed on the Duck Boat ride instead.

83.

"Who are you?" said the squirrel chained to the tree branch. Jolly looked up. It asked him, "Who set you free?" Then the rabbit turned around and begged, "Please can you let us go too?" Jolly said, "I'm sorry. I don't know how. I hope I'm just passing through." High up on the wall, the cuckoo in the clock fluttered her locked wings. "You can do it," she chirped. "Push the red button on the piano keys."

84.

Every late morning Mike Edwards arrived for work. Sometimes the Fun Forest was covered in dew like it walked with a raincoat in the early dawn. Mike started here during the World's Fair back in '62 and he knew every ride. But in all his years he never pushed the Bonanza's red button. It was forbidden, it was only there for an emergency. At the start of his shift when he pulled a switch, everything began to move. He never thought of the animals as being alive like him.

85.

Thirty years in a carnival and Mike Edwards had seen it all, or so he said. One long day turned into night. He took tickets, and if somebody won, they got a prize. Everything in his sight was controlled as a tidepool. Then again, it only took one big splash to send out waves. You had to stay alert. Mike was halfway through a cigarette and this week's *Wise Penny* when it happened.

86.

The dead wooden hands of the piano player hovered and shook over the keyboard as Jolly dashed across. Some guns trained on him, but he wasn't easy to hit. He landed on the red button and jumped up and down until it worked. Every Bonanza trap or chain that kept an animal target locked in place suddenly released. People screamed as those prisoners ran at them or flew with ragged wings over the counter into the falling night.

87.

Jolly found himself flying too. He couldn't see who held him in the air, the fur behind his neck was clutched by little carved feet. Goodbye Bonanza! It was gone like a bad dream. "You did it!" cried the cuckoo. "I knew you could!" She carried him as far as her painted wings could, to another perch above the crowds, safe from bullets and thrown balls, at the very top of the Flight to Mars.

88.

The Fun Forest jeweled around him. All the colored lights were going on. The Ferris wheel spun against a purple sky. Jolly watched from the peak of a black witch's hat. It was set on her giant green head and it rocked gently back and forth as she laughed. She was the queen of outer space, she really had seen it all, every joy and folly and twist of fate, and all she could do was laugh.

89.

A moose walked free among everyone. He wore a few wooden slats around his neck and some plaster stuck to his horns. Scars and patches covered him. Since 1962, he could only stand with his head in the wall and talk, talk, talk, as if anyone was listening. Finally someone was. He was let go, released just like a thistle on the wind, and wherever he chose to plant his feet would be his new home.

90.

Lila was back under blackberries and except for the glow of a candle, it was night. She never really saw the person who had taken pity on her, it was his way to stay out of sight as much as possible and she could understand that. Weasels weren't that different. She heard pages turn every minute or so. He was reading a book that their reality bent around, she and the world, their senses only filtered through him like sand.

91.

Surely you can tell this story is going to somewhere with a warm ending. I promised as much, didn't I? Let's hope so. The world as we know it is changing every day. I wish we could stop all the wars and realize all we have to do is care for each other. Everything we do has an effect on the planet. Where else can we go? No rocket ark is big enough to carry everyone away.

92.

Jolly spent his first night alone apart from his family up in a witch's hat. The Fun Forest became dark and finally almost silent. Like a real forest, not everything slept, but Jolly did. What a long tiring day it had been. His dream floated across the city and found Lila and Jack and the three of them were in the same dream, so real they knew they would be alright.

93.

What about Jack and the pigeons? The birds all returned to the rooftop, to the cage they lived in. They looked all over town and they asked other birds and even a policeman's horse. They spread the word, but no one had seen the two weasels. The pigeons settled in for the night and Jack shut their latch and he went to sit on the ledge. Funny, his eyes roamed right over where Jolly and Lila slept in the dark.

94.

Before you fall asleep, do you ever close your eyes and look for where dreams begin? Like any dark path that's overgrown, that tugs you with branches and thorns, it isn't easy to do, to get through all the thoughts and glimpses in your way. Your mind will make distractions as you stare at the black. Keep going. It takes a while for your troubling thoughts to become no more than little stars in a vast outer space.

95.

The morning came to everyone. Lila, Jolly, Jack, the trees and roofs and windows and the streetsweeper who was up with the birds. They started singing the day almost mechanically like the wooden cuckoo from the Fun Forest clock. There's a bird with things to do. First, she flew to Mars, not the planet, that would be too far, she flew to the neon sign, the rusted top of the letter M where she waited for Jolly to wake.

96.

"Good morning…" Jack stretched and reached for Lila and felt only air. His hand that was used to her shoulder or hip hovered 14 stories above the ground. He caught himself from falling off, somehow he forgot where he was, on the rooftop ledge of the Leopold, not the dream he thought he was in, but somewhere else.

97.

Sparrows and other finches hopped about the vines getting their breakfast. Their happy sounds, and the drops of dew they made fall with each jump along the thorns, and the flicks they made of daylight and shadow, stirred Lila from sleep. For a little while she lay in bed and watched the bird movie, the way I did when I was a kid when I would stay home from school and have soup and watch black and white movies until I was better.

98.

My friend Aaron also remembers a day like that. When he was too sick for third grade, *Billy the Kid Versus Dracula* kept him company. Monsters had a power over us in those days. It only seemed natural to check out their books at the library, to draw them, and wait for them to appear on TV. When you're young and dipped into this world, the stories you're told are the feathers that help you to fly.

99.

"You're going to be okay now," he told her. "That arm is good as new." Lila removed the bandage and brushed off the leaf and poultice and it was true. "I don't think it was really broken," he said, "It only felt that way." To her, it felt like magic. When you are all better, after something was terribly wrong, the world is a miracle and you are its song.

100.

It wasn't the sun or the sound of a broom on the damp concrete, not the crows or the gulls that tracked in the air—what woke up Jolly was a rare bird, a cuckoo telling him it was seven o'clock. Time to get up. Time to move off the witch's hat on the Flight to Mars, time to leave the Fun Forest before it started again. It was time that was ticking towards somewhere to be.

101.

Just because this book is moving closer to a Wizard of Oz ending doesn't mean the weasels will always live that way. Nobody can. Bad things come along just as surely as good things. That's how it goes. There will be times after this book is over when the Worrys will have troubles again, but that isn't this story. For now, let's let them be happy.

102.

This next time the pigeons came back, they carried good news. Then they bunched together and they carried Jack. If you ever need help finding something you lost, ask a bird. They're always listening. And when they sing, that's their radio. This morning was a melody so catchy it was passed from wing to wing and by the afternoon it was a gold record on the wall.

103.

Lila was done with the cardboard box. She held on with both hands to the metal prow of the shopping cart as it cut between cars and parking lots, over potholes in alleys, shadows and puddles and patches of concrete where the morning sunshine flared. She was nautical and leading the way like the carved figurehead of a sailing ship pointed forward into the waves.

104.

Picture a magic carpet only instead of sheep's wool dyed with indigo leaves and larkspur, pigeons are keeping it in the air and riding like Aladdin on all that undulation is Mr. Worry, cheering and whooping like someone on a roller coaster. This was his first time on a pigeon taxi. It took him across the city, tracing over the map of it. Jack got to see the sights like a tourist.

105.

If you live in this city, you see pigeons. They're part of the powerlines, the rooftops aerials, fire escapes, parks and sidewalks, the skyline they cross all day long. The Leopold roof is home to Pigeon Taxi. They've been in the phonebook since 2010, right after the listing for Pig Iron Casting & Molding located west of the interstate, on Lincoln Street.

106.

It's a little amazing the things people don't notice. Did you know at the very moment the pigeons were taxiing Jack, right below in broad daylight on 45th, a moose clopped along the sidewalk. Jolly called out from its back, seven feet in the air, and nobody heard. His voice existed in the ultrasonic low frequency where the whales and elephants talk to each other.

107.

The Bonanza moose spotted the Blackberry Maniac—I mean, John—on the hill pushing his grocery cart beyond Aurora Avenue. Jolly jumped up and down in the antlers and called out, "Mom! Mom!" but the traffic noise was drowning him out. At least he knew they were almost there. The moose was nimble as a salmon swimming upstream between the rapids of cars.

108.

Forty years ago, I rode my bike along this same path. When I was a kid, I went to the park with my friend and we would pretend to time travel and look for dinosaurs in the woods. We climbed branches and slid down the ravine and hid from pterodactyls and mastodons. With my imagination going like a movie, I wouldn't be surprised by a weasel riding a moose. I bet I would have seen them, I bet I still would.

109.

The pigeons, the grocery cart, and the invisible moose all met in the park. Lila, Jack and Jolly were together again. What a relief! What a joy! The Worrys didn't have to worry anymore! They had the perfect world to live in and a hollow tree spire nearly tall as the Leopold with room at the top for a wooden bird from a cuckoo clock. I guess this is a pretty good place to stop. I guess we can say: The End.

The WORRYS
Writing:
9/18/22—10/29/22

Fred Sodt sketch for *Kennedy* (2018)

Books by Good Deed Rain

Saint Lemonade, Allen Frost, 2014. Two novels illustrated by the author in the manner of the old Big Little Books.

Playground, Allen Frost, 2014. Poems collected from seven years of chapbooks.

Roosevelt, Allen Frost, 2015. A Pacific Northwest novel set in July, 1942, when a boy and a girl search for a missing elephant. Illustrated throughout by Fred Sodt.

5 Novels, Allen Frost, 2015. Novels written over five years, featuring circus giants, clockwork animals, detectives and time travelers.

The Sylvan Moore Show, Allen Frost, 2015. A short story omnibus of 193 stories written over 30 years.

Town in a Cloud, Allen Frost, 2015. A three-part book of poetry, written during the Bellingham rainy seasons of fall, winter, and spring.

A Flutter of Birds Passing Through Heaven: A Tribute to Robert Sund, 2016. Edited by Allen Frost and Paul Piper. The story of a legendary Ish River poet & artist.

At the Edge of America, Allen Frost, 2016. Two novels in one book blend time travel in a mythical poetic America.

Lake Erie Submarine, Allen Frost, 2016. A two week vacation in Ohio inspired these poems, illustrated by the author.

and Light, Paul Piper, 2016. Poetry written over three years. Illustrated with watercolors by Penny Piper.

The Book of Ticks, Allen Frost, 2017. A giant collection of 8 mysterious adventures featuring Phil Ticks. Illustrated throughout by Aaron Gunderson.

I Can Only Imagine, Allen Frost, 2017. Five adventures of love and heartbreak dreamed in an imaginary world. Cover & color illustrations by Annabelle Barrett.

The Orphanage of Abandoned Teenagers, Allen Frost, 2017. A fictional guide for teens and their parents. Illustrated by the author.

In the Valley of Mystic Light: An Oral History of the Skagit Valley Arts Scene, 2017. A comprehensive illustrated tribute. Edited by Claire Swedberg & Rita Hupy.

Different Planet, Allen Frost, 2017. Four science fiction adventures: reincarnation, robots, talking animals, outer space and clones. Illustrated by Laura Vasyutynska.

Go with the Flow: A Tribute to Clyde Sanborn, 2018. Edited by Allen Frost. The life and art of a timeless river poet. In beautiful living color!

Homeless Sutra, Allen Frost, 2018. Four stories: Sylvan Moore, a flying monk, a water salesman, and a guardian rabbit.

The Lake Walker, Allen Frost 2018. A little novel set in black and white like one of those old European movies about death and life.

A Hundred Dreams Ago, Allen Frost, 2018. A winter book of poetry and prose. Illustrated by Aaron Gunderson.

Almost Animals, Allen Frost, 2018. A collection of linked stories, thinking about what makes us animals.

The Robotic Age, Allen Frost, 2018. A vaudeville magician and his faithful robot track down ghosts. Illustrated throughout by Aaron Gunderson.

Kennedy, Allen Frost, 2018. This sequel to *Roosevelt* is a coming-of-age fable set during two weeks in 1962 in a mythical Kennedyland. Illustrated throughout by Fred Sodt.

Fable, Allen Frost, 2018. There's something going on in this country and I can best relate it in fable: the parable of the rabbits, a bedtime story, and the diary of our trip to Ohio.

Elbows & Knees: Essays & Plays, Allen Frost, 2018. A thrilling collection of writing about some of my favorite subjects, from B-movies to Brautigan.

The Last Paper Stars, Allen Frost 2019. A trip back in time to the 20 year old mind of Frankenstein, and two other worlds of the future.

Walt Amherst is Awake, Allen Frost, 2019. The dreamlife of an office worker. Illustrated throughout by Aaron Gunderson.

When You Smile You Let in Light, Allen Frost, 2019. An atomic love story written by a 23 year old.

Pinocchio in America, Allen Frost, 2019. After 82 years buried underground, Pinocchio returns to life behind a car repair shop in America.

Taking Her Sides on Immortality, Robert Huff, 2019. The long awaited poetry collection from a local, nationally renowned master of words.

Florida, Allen Frost, 2019. Three days in Florida turned into a book of sunshine inspired stories.

Blue Anthem Wailing, Allen Frost, 2019. My first novel written in college is an apocalyptic, Old Testament race through American shadows while Amelia Earhart flies overhead.

The Welfare Office, Allen Frost, 2019. The animals go in and out of the office, leaving these stories as footprints.

Island Air, Allen Frost, 2019. A detective novel featuring haiku, a lost library book and streetsongs.

Imaginary Someone, Allen Frost, 2020. A fictional memoir featuring 45 years of inspirations and obstacles in the life of a writer.

Violet of the Silent Movies, Allen Frost, 2020. A collection of starry-eyed short story poems, illustrated by the author.

The Tin Can Telephone, Allen Frost, 2020. A childhood memory novel set in 1975 Seattle, illustrated by author.

Heaven Crayon, Allen Frost, 2020. How the author's first book *Ohio Trio* would look if printed as a Big Little Book. Illustrated by the author.

Old Salt, Allen Frost, 2020. Authors of a fake novel get chased by tigers. Illustrations by the author.

A Field of Cabbages, Allen Frost, 2020. The sequel to *The Robotic Age* finds our heroes in a race against time to save Sunny Jim's ghost. Illustrated by Aaron Gunderson.

River Road, Allen Frost, 2020. A paperboy delivers the news to a ghost town. Illustrated by the author.

The Puttering Marvel, Allen Frost, 2021. Eleven short stories with illustrations by the author.

Something Bright, Allen Frost, 2021. 106 short story poems walking with you from winter into spring. Illustrated by the author.

The Trillium Witch, Allen Frost, 2021. A detective novel about witches in the Pacific Northwest rain. Illustrated by the author.

Cosmonaut, Allen Frost, 2021. Yuri Gagarin's rocket lands in America. Midnight jazz, folk music, mystery and sorcery. Illustrated by the author.

Thriftstore Madonna, Allen Frost, 2021. 124 summer story poems. Illustrated by the author.

Half a Giraffe, Allen Frost, 2021. A magical novel about a counterfeiter and his unusual, beloved pet. Illustrated by the author.

Lexington Brown & The Pond Projector, Allen Frost, 2022. An underwater invention takes three friends through time. Illustrated by Aaron Gunderson.

The Robert Huck Museum, Allen Frost, 2022. The artist's life story told in photographs, woodcuts, paintings, prints and drawings.

Mrs. Magnusson & Friends, Allen Frost, 2022. A collection of 13 stories featuring mystery and ginkgo leaves.

Magic Island, Allen Frost, 2022. There's a memory machine in this magical novel that takes us to college.

A Red Leaf Boat, Allen Frost, 2022. Inspired by Japan, this book of 142 poems is the result of walking in autumn.

Forest & Field, Allen Frost, 2022. 117 forest and field recordings made during the summer months, ending with a lullaby.

The Wires and Circuits of Earth, Allen Frost, 2022. 11 stories from a train station pulp magazine.

The Air Over Paris, Allen Frost, 2023. This novel reveals the truth about semi-sentient speedbumps from Mars.

Neptunalia, Allen Frost, 2023. A movie-novel for Neptune, featuring mystery in a Counterfeit Reality machine. Illustrated by Aaron Gunderson.

The Worrys, Allen Frost, 2023. A family of weasels look for a better life and get it. Illustrated by Tai Vugia.

Books by Bottom Dog Press

Ohio Trio, Allen Frost, 2001. Three short novels written in magic fields and small towns of Ohio. Reprinted as *Heaven Crayon* in 2020.

Bowl of Water, Allen Frost, 2004. Poetry. From the glass factory to when you wake up.

Another Life, Allen Frost, 2007. Poetry. From the last Ohio morning to the early bird.

Home Recordings, Allen Frost, 2009. Poetry. Dream machinery, filming Caruso, benign time travel.

The Mermaid Translation, Allen Frost, 2010. A bathysphere novel with Philip Marlowe.

Selected Correspondence of Kenneth Patchen, Edited by Larry Smith and Allen Frost, 2012. Amazing artist letters.

The Wonderful Stupid Man, Allen Frost, 2012. Short stories go from Aristotle's first Car to the $500 dollar fool.

p.s.

A racoon came round the corner of 48th. His arms were full. He was tired carrying their things. It was a long way from the tree where the weasels took off on their adventure. Do you think it was easy for a racoon to track them down? Think of all the streets and avenues and parks and the aqueduct and monorail tracks. There are a million places they could go. The address on their bag only read: 'The Worrys, Somewhere Safe.' Finally, a bird showed him where that was.

Ingram Content Group UK Ltd.
Milton Keynes UK
UKHW041221130623
423369UK00001B/2

9 781088 121689